The Trustee's Handbook

Ten Rules for New Church Leaders

The Trustee's Handbook

Ten Rules for New Church Leaders

Douglas Scaddan Publishing

The Trustee's Handbook Copyright © 2019 Douglas Scaddan

All rights reserved. No part of this book may be reproduced in any form or by any electronic or mechanical means, including information storage and retrieval systems, without written permission from the author, except in the case of a reviewer, who may quote brief passages embodied in critical articles or in a review.

This is a work of fiction. Names, characters, places, and incidents either are the product of the author's imagination or are used fictitiously, and any resemblance to actual persons, living or dead, events, or locales is entirely coincidental.

Published by Douglas Scaddan Publishing
1st Printing 2013
2nd Printing 2019

ISBN: 978-0-9683071-5-1

Calling All Church Leaders

This is the book you've been looking for! No, seriously it is. Have you ever looked at some church politics and felt shame on their behalf? Have you ever seen people's egos get in the way of God's plans? Have you seen some decision that made you wonder just who was really in charge?

This book is for you. The man behind the table serving, but no one really knows his name. The woman who cleans the communion cups, and teaches Sunday school.

This book is also for all those people that think that Robert's Rules should be part of the Canon.

Praise for The Trustee's Manual

    The author's knowledge and application of scriptures makes The Trustee's Manuel indispensable for basic trustee training. His experience and research enables an informed presentation delivered in an engaging style. Purposefully, he removes lingering doubts about the spiritual role of Christians entrusted with civic stewardship on behalf of congregations. Believers will be able to grasp the essential role of trustee without feeling the need to be a bible scholar. I highly recommend this gem.

    - Samuel (Amazon.com user)

Praise for The Janitor

This book may be a work of fiction, but the voice of Scaddan's narrative makes it feel as real as my own life. I was challenged by this book, reintroduced to the love of God and simple faith, and filled with tears as I related to the pains and joys of my new friends off these pages. I recommend this book to anyone who can spare a few minutes for a short read.

- Josh (Amazon.ca user)

Dedication

For the only One that is worthy of Glory.
If I have to tell you who that is, you need more help than I can give.

Acknowledgments

My mind is full of so many people that have molded me through the years. My parents, my friends, roll models that I have tried to emulate. It took many years, but I finally found that one thing that I really needed. God made me just the way I am. The least I can do is be the man He made me to be.

The greatest man of God I ever knew is a semi retired Baptist preacher from West Virginia.
His name is Michael Sullivan.

Also by Douglas Scaddan Publishing

The Soldiers of God
The Janitor
The Lightbringer

Introduction

    I started writing this manual mainly as something for myself. The ten rules that Trustees should follow. I saw that the church today was so engrossed in the politics and "corporate" running of the day to day church that they had forgotten the basics that had already been laid out for them in the Bible. So, one afternoon, I sat down and wrote ten rules. To me they are obvious rules. I was a new Trustee in my small church and perhaps I was full of the excitement and fervor that changing the world for Christ had in my mind. Was I ever wrong!

    My church was full of politics and interpersonal disputes and mislaid priorities. Then, a couple weeks after I had been voted to the Board of Trustees, I was made the Chairman of the Board of Trustees. I was sickened by what I read in the past minutes, the condition of the budget and the priorities by which the Trustees ran the corporate aspect of the church. I took a couple of months and talked to men and women that I trusted and looked up to spiritually, I bounced ideas off them and received feedback. I asked questions and I prayed. LORD HOW I PRAYED!! I read my Bible, I studied it, I became an expert in what the Bible said that new churches were run like. Then, I prayed some more. It was then that I discovered that I was a moron. A church in the first century could not possibly be compared with a church in the twenty-first century with any kind of comparable data, besides, of course, the one link that is the important one, our faith in Christ.

    So I sat down one afternoon and wrote the ten rules that are here. This manuscript is by a trustee, for a trustee, or a church in general. If you're looking for deep and life altering insight into the Bible, go get another book. I am not a scholar, and I don't try to be one. I say what needs to be said and that's all. The rules laid out here are, in my mind, logical ones that should have been self evident from the start.

I talked to people that I trust and look up to spiritually and try to emulate their Christian walk. People that are gentle and kind and make me think of Christ when I see them or talk to them. I asked them about the rules and what they thought of them. Some gave me feedback and some gave me positive encouragement. The feedback I then took and prayed about, and studied other manuscripts of this type. After about two years of this I came up with these 10 rules. They have changed, been revised, altered, and any number of different things have happened to them. Some of the harder rules to follow I struggled over whether or not to even keep them. But the purpose of a lesson is to teach, and I firmly believe that these lessons are from God.

They are simple rules, and some will make you say, "Well that makes sense." Others will make you upset or downright angry. I shall explain each one in detail later, first let me introduce you to the rules.

RULE 1
Everything we do is for the benefit of the Kingdom of God.
RULE 2
The bricks, mortar, carpets, pews, drywall and the light bulbs all belong to God.
RULE 3
There is no separation of Ministry and Business. Ministry IS the Business.
RULE 4
Marketing - No one will come to listen to anybody preach if no one knows he or she is talking.
RULE 5
Planning a budget is like forecasting your own success or failure, and should be approached carefully.
RULE 6
Change your community before you try to change the world. Take a good long look at what needs to be done and do it!

RULE 7
If it's good and right and Biblical, do it! If it doesn't meet all three of those criteria, then don't.

RULE 8
The Pastor leads the Ministry. Ministry is the business of the Church. Trustees run the business side of the church, therefore, the Pastor LEADS the Trustees, not commands, leads. (I'll explain in detail later.)

RULE 9
Bylaws are GUIDELINES! The Bible is the Law

RULE 10
Thank God for everything. If you can't find something to thank Him for then listen to your heart.

That's it. Ten basic rules in a nutshell. If you haven't thrown this manuscript out the window or are not right now trying to find out where I live so you can lynch me I'll assume you want to read more. In the first chapter we'll explore what a Trustee board is and then we'll go into detail to each rule chapter by chapter. I trust and pray that this will be helpful to you, in some way, big or small.

Douglas Scaddan

So You Were Dumb Enough to Say Yes, Now What?

Alright, so I'm having some fun with the title of this chapter. Being a Trustee should be a fun and rewarding experience. What I mean is the very word Trustee means that YOU have been trusted with the legal, and financial operations of GOD's property! See Rule number two. You'll find that all the Rules are very interactive with each other and as we go through them I'll point out the interactions that they have with one another. Rule One and Rule Ten are pretty much universal with all the Rules, but they all are related in some way with each other.

As I said before being a Trustee should be fun and rewarding. The day after I found out that I was voted to the Board of Trustees I was talking to a friend of mine who said, "I'm sorry to hear that. Get ready for the biggest test of faith you've ever faced!" When I was voted Chairman I was told by the same friend, "You're in for fight after fight." It didn't sound like fun to me. But I discovered that as long as priorities are kept straight and that we keep our eyes on the prize, being a trustee can be a rewarding, fun, and spiritually moving job.

First off we should probably have a definition of two things, one is Church Leader. A church leader is someone, within your local congregation that people naturally look towards for spiritual guidance and direction. They are generally people that have a magnetic personality and that people stop and listen to when he/she talks. The second definition that we need is for a

Church Trustee. A trustee should be a church leader, with added responsibilities. A trustee is a person that has been selected by the congregation to handle the legal and financial responsibilities of the local congregation "in trust" for God.

In most church models a Board of Trustees is made up of 4 to 8 individuals aged 40 to 10 years younger than God. The church Treasurer and the Pastor also sit in as non-voting "advisory" members. For a normal Board meeting you'll go through bland stuff like approving maintenance expenditures and changes to the contracts for building rentals, money income, and spending and a whole lot of boring stuff.

Make no mistake, this stuff is important for a modern church. Churches now need to maintain a certain legal responsibility as well as the charges given to us by Jesus Christ. Remember what Jesus said, "Give the government what is theirs, and give God what is His." Okay, so I paraphrased that. But wait! You say, everything belongs to God! Yes it does, but it belongs to God whether or not we send it to the government or fill in the paperwork for non-profit status, or if we ensure that the building is up to code.

Weak Boards will be run by the Pastor or the Treasurer, or by particularly "loud" Board members, while Boards that have a number of strong minded individuals will get very little done, unless they all have the same heart for Jesus that we all should. This is why I have these Rules laid out before you, to avoid both problems. Let's try to be realistic here, interpersonal interactions and people's own sense of right and wrong are going to effect any kind of decision that is made in a group setting. Keeping our eyes on the goal, the building up of the Kingdom of God MUST be foremost on our minds when we approach decisions as stewards of God's church. But what about rules that might already be in place?

Board meetings are generally run by Robert's Rules, which was written by a guy a long time ago when it was common for people to carry side arms. If you have a copy of this book, throw it out. If a church Trustee meeting needs a book to tell them how to play nice with each other you have bigger problems then how to run a meeting. I don't believe that God wants the Body of Christ to interact with each other based on a series of rules laid down by someone that wasn't Him. He wants us to love each other, be kind to one another and show each other respect and politeness.

Not that you shouldn't have an agenda or keep minutes, those are legal requirements for most non-profit organizations, but if the chair of the Board is ready to start the meeting he shouldn't have to "Call the Meeting to Order", "Hey guys let's get started" should suffice. Remember we're all brothers and sisters in Christ here. Bob shouldn't need to be recognized to "Have the floor", you should all be polite enough to let him talk. Everyone has a say, everyone has a voice that should be listened to, and respected as no one, not me or you, can pick and choose who God will speak through.

The Chair should, however, maintain constant control of the flow of the meeting. Some topics can get pretty touchy, sadly it's generally where money is concerned and the chair needs to see these dynamics in the meeting and react appropriately. If a discussion is getting out of hand then call an immediate vote to finish it or table it to another meeting, perhaps a special meeting for that topic alone. These things shouldn't affect the personal relationships of the people involved.

Every meeting should start and finish with prayer. Rule number three. Pray for each other, pray for the meeting or pray for the community, but pray. Let the Holy Spirit lead you, the meeting, and your decisions, but pray. Pray individually during the meeting and especially before a vote. Pray, pray again, and then pray some more. Give the controls to Christ and never, take them back during the whole meeting. Surrender all to Him who is worthy. It is a hard bit of advice to do, but I learned that from the wisest man I know, a Southern Baptist Minister, named Rev. M.L. Sullivan, that has planted 3 churches and mentored more people to closer relationships to Christ then I can count. If I become half the man of God he is, I will be a happy man.

Our particular church model has two major groups. The Trustees, which care for the boring legal stuff and the Church Counsel, which takes care of ministry and worship and all the fun stuff. The major challenge with this model, (and I don't think there is a model that doesn't have some kind of major challenge) is that you have two different "camps", the "Realists" (Trustees) and the "Dreamers", (Counsel). There should be a great deal of communication between these two groups if there is to be any kind of real work to be done. The main thrust of communication once again falls on the chair of the Trustees, who gets to attend both meetings. (Lucky guy eh?) Communication must be a priority in any church. Every part of the Body of Christ is important, 1 Corinthians 12:12-26 talks about that. Take a minute to reflect on how best to apply it in your church.

For even as the body is one and yet has many members, and all the members of the body, though they are many, are one body, so also is Christ. For by one Spirit we were all baptized into one body, whether Jews or Greeks, whether slaves or free, and we were all made to drink of one Spirit. For the body is not one member, but many. If the foot says, "Because I am not a hand, I am not a part of the body," it is not for this reason any the less a part of the body. And if the ear says, "Because I am not an eye, I am not a part of the body," it is not for this reason any the less a part of the body. If the whole body were an eye, where would the hearing be? If the whole were hearing, where would the sense of smell be? But now God has placed the members, each one of them, in the body, just as He desired. If they were all one member, where would the body be? But now there are many members, but one body. And the eye cannot say to the hand, "I have no need of you"; or again the head to the feet, "I have no need of you." On the contrary, it is much truer that the members of the body which seem to be weaker are necessary; and those members of the body which we deem less honorable, on these we bestow more abundant honor, and our less presentable members become much more presentable, whereas our more presentable members have no need of it. But God has so composed the body, giving more abundant honor to that member which lacked, so that there may be no division in the body, but that the members may have the same care for one another. And if one member suffers, all the members suffer with it; if one member is honored, all the members rejoice with it. (NIV)

Remarkably, I hadn't been on any voted board or committee before and there I was, chair of the trustees. Everyone looked to me for decisions. People that I had never talked to before beyond "Hi" and "How are you?" were now approaching me with questions or comments about this or that. I would smile and nod and in the end say something like, "Well is it in the budget?" or "Is it the right thing to do in the eyes of God?" I was terrified. What I should have been asking in those first few months was, "What do you think?" or "Do you have any ideas of how to do that?" God gave us an entire Body to work with, different people with different views and different outlooks. Perhaps in those places we might find a diamond, an idea, or an answer to a difficult question that none had thought of before.

The main focus should not be with the Trustees, the council, or whatever you call them in your church. The main focus should be the work of God. The dreamers dream and the realists tell the dreamers if it can happen. Keeping in mind, of course, the priorities that Christ would have were He here. The church leadership should be listening to people that go to them with their questions or ideas. It's the church leadership that's responsible for organizing outreach and local ministry. It's the church pastor that equips everyone in the church to do the work that the church is actually there for! The Trustees? As part of the church leadership, they are part of that rewarding and biblically commanded part of the church. Matthew 28:19 - 20. Go ahead, look it up.

We are all here to do the will of God in all things that we do! Whether you're a council member, a member of the trustees, chair of the board of trustees, or the guy that sits in the third pew from the back! YOU are here to do the will of God. Don't ever think that you are JUST the guy that signs the cheques, changes the light-bulbs, or polishes the pews with that pine scented stuff. You are a vital and important part of the Kingdom of God, don't let ANYONE tell you differently! Hey, chances are I don't know you, or have even met you, but I know that God has plans for you! How do I know this? The Bible says so, in Jeremiah 29: 11, "For I know the plans I have for you, declares the Lord, plans to prosper you and not to harm you, plans to give you hope and a future." (NIV) God knows the plan, not you nor I. God. And He has plans for you, specifically. Don't let anyone tell you you're JUST whatever, especially not you!

Rule Number One: Let's Get Our Priorities Straight

The Bible proves absolutely nothing besides the fact that it was, at one time, written down. If this statement angers you or gets your back up it tells me two things, One, that you view the Bible as the written word of God and that it has a special place in your heart. Two, that you have faith in that written word. This is good, we can now move on to the reading of the Bible with the understanding that we all have faith that it is the written word of God and that it is Truth in word. If you read that first statement and didn't get at least bothered by it, then I can't help you in this book and you should go talk to your pastor.

It is faith that is the basic push of the Bible. Faith in the Bible as being true, faith in God, faith that Jesus rose from the grave after dying to set us free from sin, and faith that He sent the Holy Spirit to guide us along this path that we've chosen. Jesus even said it Himself. "Whoever has FAITH in me will be saved." Okay, so I paraphrased that from John 3:16.

So Rule number one says that "Everything we do is for the benefit of the Kingdom of God". Great so let's define the Kingdom of God for those of us that don't know.

The Kingdom of God is mentioned in the Bible by Jesus in a bunch of places from Matthew to John, in a number of different contexts and wordings. We use the words of Jesus here because it's always important to take the words of Jesus as the final authority on all things. For this particular discussion I'll be working from Luke. So go and get your Bible and read Luke 17:20-21. No really, put this down and go and get your Bible and read it. It's the book after Mark. I'll wait.

So you've read it right? It says, "Once having been asked by the Pharisees when the Kingdom of God would come, Jesus replied, 'The Kingdom of God does not come with your careful observation, nor will people say, 'Here it is,' or 'There it is,' because the Kingdom of God is within you.'". (Luke 17:20-21, NIV) So there you have it. The Kingdom of God is within you! Another translation for within could be among. Either way you look at it, the Kingdom of God is here and now!!!

Let's look at another part of that passage. Jesus also says that the Kingdom of God does not come with "careful observation". What does that mean? It means that the Kingdom of God is not something that makes itself known by stagnant waiting. That is, sitting around twiddling your thumbs and saying to yourself, "The Kingdom of God is going to be here. Any minute now . . . any minute now." A friend of mine, Pastor Harry Hoehne, also made sure, in my early draft of this that I made the distinction of "prayerful anticipation". The primary word there is prayerful. You're still doing something. You're praying! You're going before God and asking, BEGGING, on your knees for Him to show His glory in the world and to bring His Kingdom to fruition! That said it should be obvious that the Kingdom of God is participatory. It's an active part of us. It requires action on our part. It's a movement that needs us to make a conscious decision to work on its behalf.

So with that in mind we must make decisions, as Trustees, to work on behalf of the Kingdom of God, to make it visible to others. The passage also talks about people not saying "Here it is,", or "There it is,". People cannot see the Kingdom of God on their own, they must be led. We, as leaders of the church MUST lead. We must guide people to Christ, or at least our decisions must.

I want to pause here and define the term, "leading to Christ". When I think about leading I immediately think of the whole "leading a horse to water" thing. That is kind of appropriate here. You can lead a horse to water, it's pretty easy, you take the horse by the lead and walk it over to the water. You cannot, however make the horse drink. I would like to see someone try one day, I think it would be amusing to watch someone try to push the horse's head down towards the trough. The same thing applies here, you can guide a person to Christ, but you cannot make them believe or have faith, that's their decision. You can, however pray that God will soften their heart or speak to them. It is not your strength or your arguments that brings about faith, it is the quiet, gentle touch of the Holy Spirit that does that.

I have done a lot of things in my life that I'm not proud of. The thing that makes me lie awake at night is this. It was at the end of a Sunday morning service and I had to talk to so and so about such and such, it was a Trustee matter and I was looking for that person. I saw the person I was looking for and made a beeline for them. I brushed by a lady and moved on. It registered in my brain that the lady was new, we have a very small church. I never saw her again.

Maybe if I had stopped and said, "Hi.". Maybe if I had at least smiled, or waved or shook her hand, or stopped and talked. It's not really the lack of action on my part that bothers me. The thing that bothers me is that I didn't even think about it until I noticed she wasn't there the following week. My lack of attitude, controlled my decisions. I didn't think so I didn't stop.

What needed to change was simple. My attitude had to be all about the Kingdom of God, in my work, in my marriage, in my actions with my children. Everything had to be for that. By no means am I perfect now, but I have recognized the problem and TOGETHER, Jesus and I, we can fix it.

How does this stuff apply to Trustees? We don't have anything to do with Ministry? No offense intended but if that's what you think you're greatly mistaken. Take a gander at Rule #3. We all work for the glory of the Kingdom of God. ALL. That means everyone. That includes Trustees. That's includes you. NO one is exempt. Get it? If you don't believe me then listen to what Jesus said in the Great Commission. It's the last few lines in Matthew. I'd love for someone one day to give a sermon about the first and last words of Jesus in each Gospel, I think that would be a powerful sermon. Then again I hope for no famine or no wars too.

We, as Trustees are to run the church as Jesus ran His ministry. He had a Treasurer, and he obviously had to eat and drink, but anything else was spent on the poor and the people who needed it. Imagine the world, if we actually helped the people around us who needed it. A lot of the time I'm willing to bet that we don't even see the problems around us. There are people in Canada and the U.S. that go hungry. Children that go to school with empty bellies, shoes a size too small and no coat. That's not even considering the fact that in the fifties and sixties the big problems in school were talking and gum chewing. Now we have metal detectors in some school to ensure that the kids don't bring firearms to school.

Clean your own backyard before you try to clean someone else's.

That's Rule #6.

Don't try to change the world, that's Jesus job. Change your life, and by doing that you'll change the lives of those around you. Use the church to change the lives of those around you that don't believe. THAT is the Kingdom of God. Showing love to ALL. The Great Commandment and the Great Commission being followed in one place. Can you imagine the kind of church that would be? Can you imagine the lives that would change if that church actually followed what Jesus said instead of making their own decisions? Think about it.

Rule Number Two: It all belongs to God

So Rule number two says, "The bricks, mortar, carpets, pews, drywall and the light bulbs all belong to God."

Seems like something that should be easy to figure out, right? Like why in the world is he putting this down, EVERYONE knows that the church belongs to God! Everyone may know that the church belongs to God but everyone may not ACT like the church belongs to God. There is a significant difference between knowing and acting. These differences can turn up with damaging consequences, let me tell you a story.

I had a friend, whom was on the board of trustees for his church. A group of people, a local charity, wanted to use the basement of their church for a drop in centre for youth. They wanted to re-fit the kitchen of the church to an industrial standard kitchen for free, pay the church's standard rental fee and take on a portion of the insurance, should the insurance go up. Nice deal eh?

The board turned it down because the kids might damage the drywall. True story. They may know the church belongs to God, but they did not act like it did.

I know most of the board members of that church, and I trust their opinions on the Bible and I seek them for prayer and advice on how to walk my Christian walk. They are people I am sure know God and have a deep relationship with Christ, but when it came to the church building they just could not let go of it and felt that it had to be protected at all cost. Even at the cost of young men and women's souls.

Some Trustees will say that it is their job to preserve the church building. That is wrong, and if someone says that to you as a job description of a Trustee, tell them this. "A Trustee's job is to use the church building in such a way to further the Great Commission and the Great Commandment. Period, end of statement, that's it, take it or leave it." There is no way that you can tell me that God needs ANYONE to protect His house.

Which brings me to my next topic, the carpet. I once went to a church where they called a special congregational meeting for two topics. The first was a decision whether or not to replace the carpet in the sanctuary. There was a spirited 90 minute discussion on the topic, pros and cons were brought forward as well as quotes from local businesses and then the pros and cons again. After the discussion the decision was made to replace the carpet. The second piece of business was a request from a local Christian who was going on missions to the Philippines to translate Bibles to the languages of the local tribes there. He was asking for money to help this mission. He was not asked to come to give a presentation and after the rather lackluster 5 minute discussion he was turned down because the church couldn't afford it.

Is it just me or is there something wrong with this picture? The carpet was okay, from what I could see. There were a few faded parts from people walking down the main aisle and such, but it seemed alright from what I could tell.

If you, right now, are thinking. "But we have to look good to bring people into the church. No one wants to go to a church that looks poor." Then I'll ask you another question. Would Jesus Christ replace the carpet or translate the Bible? Jesus taught on hillsides, as well as temples. Churches in Africa are growing and churches in Canada and the U.S. are closing. The African churches are meeting in large open areas! There are hundreds of house churches in India! Does that maybe tell you that the building isn't what's important? The message is what's important. The building is a tool. The building is just a place for the pastor to speak and not get rained on.

If you find yourself still thinking that the building is more important than the message and you're a trustee or worse yet a pastor, do this. Open your Bible like it's the first time. Find that excitement and joy that the Holy Spirit brings and read. Pray that the Spirit will guide you, don't force the issue, pray for guidance and pray for an awakening of your heart to what the Lord wants to say. Most importantly, open the Bible with no preconceived notions. Look at it like you're a child in Christ again, and soak all of what God wants to tell you into your heart.

I'm not saying don't change the carpet or look after the building, by all means that is stuff that has to be done. Just make sure you have it in it's proper perspective. Do the work of God, then do the work on the church. Do the work of God ... Hey that brings us perfectly into rule number three!

Rule Number Three: What is it we're supposed to do again?

Rule number three states, "There is no separation of Ministry and Business. Ministry IS the Business." Well that's pretty obvious, you may be thinking right about now. Let me add a little bit more to that thought. The business of the church is ministry, the trustees of a church are the legal representatives of the church, and therefore, the trustees of the church are legally responsible for the business of the church. Wild thought isn't it?

If your church happens to use the template that has a church counsel that runs the ministry portion, then I can see a bunch of you trustees right now saying, "But the counsel runs that portion of the church!" Or maybe you have a ministry committee, or a group of people that meets for coffee every Wednesday to plan ministry. It doesn't matter.

Let me break this down a little more for those people. The church trustees are legally responsible for everything that happens in the church. It is in your best interests to be as well informed of ministry as you are of the price of the insurance. And become involved in the ministry, in whatever role you can play. We can also look at it from a more traditional business perspective. The more people that are brought to Christ, the more people are sitting in your pews. The more money comes to the church, the greater the church grows. The more effective ministry becomes, the more people are brought to Christ. Ministry, and the spreading of the Word is what the lifeblood of a church is, without that all you're running is a country club for people that like to get up early on Sundays and sing and listen to your pastor talk.

Let me throw some statistics I found in James MacDonald's book, Vertical Church at you. Six Thousand churches close up shop every year. One pastor in ten will retire while still in ministry. Eight hundred new churches survive their first year. Ten thousand new churches would be needed every year to keep up with population growth. A mere 15% of churches in the United States are growing, and of those churches only 2% are effectively bringing people to Christ.

Those statistics are staggeringly scary. We, as church leaders cannot afford to just worry about keeping the business side of the church working. We must get it through our thick skulls that ministry, the act of bringing people to Christ is the business of the church! With numbers like that, which most of you trustee types should be able to understand, we are failing God on an epic scale. So, what do we do about it, you ask me with bated breath, waiting for a life altering answer. For that answer we must turn back to the Bible.

So there the early church guys were sitting around on Pentecost. Probably reading their well worn copies of Robert's Rules, right? Sorry, just kidding. Acts 2 relates the whole story, but in it we get the idea that something had changed in the world, something important, and something that would change the world. The Holy Spirit. The third facet of the unimaginably complex God, coming to rest as "tongues of fire that separated and came to rest on each of them." (Acts 2:3 NIV) This was the gift of God, given to those that believed and had faith in the Word . . . Jesus.

In Galatians 4:4-7 it talks about receiving "adoption to sonship" (Gal 4:5, NIV), and that you are "no longer a slave, but GOD'S CHILD" (Gal 4:7, NIV) We are the children of God! We are heirs to the Kingdom of God! With that sonship comes the gift of the Holy Spirit! That is exciting to me and it should be to you, you aren't just running a building where the preacher can preach, you're building the Kingdom of God! In your own backyard, in your own community! The ministries that you approve are directly responsible for the building of that Kingdom, and they should have a priority.

The business of the church is ministry and the purpose of ministry is to bring people to Christ. In Acts 2 we see that the Father laid His Spirit on the lives of the people in that small upper room and they used the Gift of the Spirit to bring 3000 people to Christ and they baptized them. (Acts 2:41,) And look at Acts 2:46 , 47, "And day by day, attending the temple together and breaking bread in their homes, they received their food with glad and generous hearts, praising God and having favour with all the people. And the Lord added to their number day by day those who were being saved."(NIV) They praised God! What a great idea! Why didn't we think of that? Let's praise God, and be thankful about our ministries. Pray about them, and try to help out with them. Give the glory to God and see what the Holy Spirit does, I'm sure the plans that God has for your church is better than your plan. No offense intended but let's be realistic, He's GOD!

Don't cut ministry because it costs too much; don't judge people because they have a Gift of Talking to Teens; don't hold people back because their Gift of Music isn't to your liking. Let the Spirit run free in your church and watch the people come to the Lord. Change the world, one person at a time. Let the Holy Spirit guide you into new, "out of the box" ministries as well. Different times and places require different methods; let the

Spirit guide you in those decisions too. I'm not saying hold onto ministries that are not effective, I'm saying give it a shot and look at it's effectiveness and then make the call. If it's changing lives for the better, then hold on to it, find the money in the budget. Bringing people to Christ is our job! If it's not effective, then find something else or tweek the existing ministry, but always, always find a way to get people the food for their souls that they need!

You say that ministry isn't the business of trustees? I tell you that ministry is the business of the church, and the church is the business of trustees. Remember? The very word "trustee" means that you have been given the church business "in trust". Don't let God down.

Rule Number Four: Didn't you tell them we were coming?

Rule number four says, "Marketing - No one will come to listen to anybody preach if no one knows he or she is talking." This is a pretty self explanatory rule. Tell people what you do at the church. Tell people about the church and tell people when you meet and what goes on. Word of mouth is the single greatest advertising plan you have at your disposal.

Marketing is best defined as creating a perception of you in a person's mind. If your church is all about singing hymns from the beginning of the 20th Century, that creates a perception. If your pastor gives his sermon while standing on a basketball, and juggling chainsaws, that's another perception. What is the perception that you want to give to your target community?

But there's more ways of creating perceptions than that, isn't there? Hold on . . . I just had to pause and imagine our pastor standing on a basketball and juggling chainsaws. You have to remember that we live in a technological world. The Internet, Facebook and Twitter all provide you with ways to get in touch with people and with the world as a whole. Those tools can also allow you to create the perception that you want to give to the community. Dynamic web-pages and cool Facebook accounts can give you great EXPOSURE, but what are you really SAYING? What is the perception that you are fostering, step back and ask yourself, What would I think if I knew nothing about Christ?

Now I can guess what some of you are saying, "But we've always done it this way! We've never used these new fangled computer, tweeting, Facebooking, internety things before!" That may be true, but I'd be willing to bet that your church has one. And if you didn't know that then there might be a problem. What is the perception that you are giving to the world. You might want to find out. Then some of you say, "Well we don't need that stuff, we've always done it this way and we don't have to change."

In response to that let me tell you a story, again.
There was a man who entered a small town and looked at the way the church was ran and said, "I've got a better way for your church to run."

The people in the town said, "We've never done it that way and we're not going to change now."

Town after town this man went, and the same thing happened over and over again. He then walked into a large city and saw the same thing, he went to the leader of the church and said, "Hey, I've got a better way of doing things! Why don't we all love each other and love God too?"

The leaders of the church, while waving copies of Robert's Rules, said, "We've always done it this way!" Then they put a crown of thorns on his head and crucified him, between two thieves, on a Friday. Need I go on?

The thing to remember is that society, culture, and the human psyche are all changing. What worked 30 years ago isn't going to work today, simply because all three of those things have changed. The human condition is a constantly adapting and fluid thing, it's one of the marvelous things that God built into us at the time of our creation; our ability to adapt. This ability to adapt has also led us to require different and more immediate means of ingesting information. The church would be silly not to make immediate use of these tools for our benefit, and the benefit of the Kingdom of God. We keep coming back to that don't we? EVERYTHING we do is for the benefit of the Kingdom of God.

The perception that we want to show the world, has not have changed. We love everyone, we worship God, and we exist to show the love of God to all. However, the way we promote those perceptions will change, in vast and differing ways as time goes on. Methodologies change but the message never does, and that is the perception that we should be sharing with the world.

When you snub a drunk that wanders into your sanctuary on Sunday morning because he is cold and wanted a place to be warm, that's a perception. When you talk about the single Mom and her two poorly dressed kids behind their back, that's a perception. And as such, that's bad marketing, despite what your web-page might say about how much you love everybody. You also want to ensure that the church is a comfortable place to be. I don't mean 300 Lazy Boys rather than pews, we all know where the bathrooms are. We all know where the nursery is. Maybe signs or a helpful tour. Make your church a second home, a comfortable and safe place to be and people will want to be there.

Twitter, Facebook and a well designed web-page are all valuable tools for a church, like it or not. Fliers, signs and posters at the local grocery store are all useful as well. Newspapers, radio spots and free event advertising (most cities have these spots on local cable or radio shows, Google it) are also useful tools. But think of this scenario. You're talking to someone about your church, you call up the church's website and Facebook page on your smart phone (everyone's got them now) and show the person where your church is, you then show the person the church's Facebook page, which allows them to get updates on church events. Then you sign them up to the church's twitter account and that's three tools that you had on your phone to provide information to your friend/co-worker/whatever.

Studies have shown that it takes a person three times to see something before they will choose to buy, or not buy. We're GIVING this stuff away! It's FREE! Eternal Life, FREE! With one conversation, you have provided all three means of information for the person and regular reminders via Facebook and Twitter. Cool isn't it?

Rule Number Five: Pull out the Crystal Ball.

Rule number five goes like this, "Planning a budget is like forecasting your own success or failure, and should be approached carefully."

Well that's a pretty silly statement isn't it? Not really, think about it. A budget predicts whether or not a church will have money at the end of the year or not. To a trustee, success is having money at the end of the year and failure is not having money at the end of the year.

This is now the point of the book where I'll tell you to go back and read Rule Number One. Everything we do is for the benefit of the Kingdom of God. Now listen to this and think for a moment, The Kingdom of God does not REQUIRE our assistance, the Kingdom of God REQUESTS our assistance. If your brain exploded, just bear with me for a moment and we'll try to put it back together.

Remember Rule One? We learned there that the Kingdom of God is here and now. What exactly is the Kingdom of God? Far smarter men than I have thought about this and written volumes of books on the topic, I like to fall back on the Bible in these cases. " And now faith, hope, and love abide, these three; and the greatest of these is love." (1 Corinthians 13:13, NRSV) This, I think, are the foundations of the Kingdom of

God, just the foundations. The idea of the Kingdom of God is so vast and so infinitesimally huge that I don't think we can ever understand it fully until we've gone Home to our reward and can ask Jesus Himself what it is. But Paul had it right, start with these three things and you can't go wrong. Faith that the Lord will provide, Hope for the future, our children, and Love for the community around us. If these three things are not taken into account when doing anything in a Trustee meeting than your time has been wasted.

And now back to your splattered brain. God doesn't require us to bring about the Kingdom of God, it's already here, remember? Besides He's GOD and He doesn't need me or anyone else to help Him if He really wants something done. He did however give us that pesky little thing called free will. We choose to follow Him, we choose to give Him the wheel and we choose to take it back more often than not.

He does hold out His hands to us and requests our assistance. He does hold out His hands to us and says, "Come to Me and I will give you rest." God is CONSTANTLY holding out His arms and saying, "Come to Me, My beloved." And He does so every second, of every day, of every month, of every year of our lives. God's good like that.

How does this apply to budgets? Did you think I just went off on some way out limb? Were you thinking, "This guy is totally off his rocker!"? Well you may be right, I am Canadian, but I'm not so far gone as to have a copy of Robert's Rules in my back pocket.

Start with a number. Not just any random number that looks good. Start with a number that has a little faith in it. I like to take last year's offerings and add 1 or 2 % in faith of the growth we should expect. Then take anything that is pretty much mandatory and issue money to it. Pastor's salary, building mortgage, upkeep and utilities, local and foreign missions, Sunday School, Christian education, music and worship and outreach are all mandatory, as well as a couple things I'm sure I forgot to mention here.

Anything left over can be placed into the extraneous expenses.

That is the easy way of doing things. Hope for the future should fall in Sunday school, Christian education, (we have to teach the new believers) and outreach (we have to get the new believers). Love, as Paul would say, is the greatest of these things. Everything we do should be done with Love. Our families, our church, our community, our city, our country, and our world; it all comes down to Love. Jesus said it best when He told us to Love one another. HE TOLD US TO DO IT! Don't tell people that Jesus loves them until YOU love them. If you have a hard time with that ask for help, I'm sure Jesus won't mind, He's good like that.

Douglas Scaddan

Rule Number Six: What do you mean we're supposed to be nice to them?

Rule six is, "Change your community before you try to change the world. Take a good long look at what needs to be done and do it!"

This is basically saying, "Do the job that Jesus told us to do!"

A lot of churches walk around with blinders on and ignore the fact that there are people who don't even know there's a church up the street. That is sad. That is a failure on a colossal scale when you look at the scorecard for the church. It may have a balanced budget and it may have a group of Christians that can quote the Bible until the cows come home. It may have pictures of missionaries in Africa and South America and other places plastered on the bulletin board that they support. They may have letters from those missionaries saying how thankful they are and that God is doing great things in those countries. That's great! That is really great and we should worship God just for that! Praise God.

That doesn't help the little boy down the street that has never known Jesus and only thinks there's a big building and a big field that he can play in at the end of his street. Who's job is it to reach him? Here's a hint, it's the person reading this manual.

The Great Commandment, which is in all the gospels, Matthew 22:36-40, Mark 12:28-33, Luke 10:25-28, and John 13:31-35, says that we should love God with all our mind, soul, and strength and that we should love our neighbor as ourselves. Since that's included in all the gospels, do you think that maybe it's pretty important?

1 Peter 4:9 says, "Be hospitable to one another without complaining." (NASB). That's pretty self explanatory, but Peter was talking to the church. So does that mean that we should only be hospitable to other Christians?

In answer to that let me refer you to the story of the Good Samaritan. (Luke 10:30-37) This is a story told to us by Jesus Christ Himself, so I guess that means it's pretty important. We all know the story, where a guy gets beat up and left on the side of the road. A Samaritan comes by and sees him and takes him to an inn, binds his wounds and pays for his food and lodging. What makes this story so great is that the Samaritans at the time were like the black sheep of the Jewish world. The Jews didn't really hang out with them and the Samaritans didn't mind. I can envision the two groups crossing the street to avoid each other, even if it took them out of the way.

And then look at what Jesus says in the last half of verse 37, "Go and do the same." Pretty simple, straightforward, and easy to understand. A command, from Jesus to us, to all of us, to go and take care of those that need it. Go love other people, even if they don't have the same political or religious views as you. Go and care for each other, no matter who they are. Go and show the love of Christ in your actions, and words. Tough? Yes. Rewarding? I can't see any commandment of Christ being less than the most rewarding thing in the universe, bar none.

Rule Number Seven: We have to read the Bible too?

Rule seven says, "If it's good and right and Biblical, do it! If it doesn't meet all three of those criteria, then don't."

I want you to try to imagine something. The Bible refers to the church as the "Body of Christ"; that's not the imagining part, that's real. (Roman's 12:4-5) We can imagine that the Body of Christ is made of individuals, us, we can also imagine that what the Bible says about an individual's body we should apply that to the Body of Christ, the church.

That said, there are a number of spots in the Bible where the actions of individuals are laid out. The best of these is, Colossians 3:15, which says, "Let the peace of Christ rule in your hearts, to which indeed you were called in one body; and be thankful."(NASB)

If this does not excite you to the point that you cannot wait until you get to church again then I don't know what more we can do. The peace of Christ in your hearts! The word of Christ richly dwelling in you! Psalms, hymns, spiritual songs, singing! And then the thing that sends shivers up my spine; Whatever you do in word or deed do all in the name of the Lord Jesus. Oh, well, I guess it's not all partying and singing and worship. We 're expected to do stuff too.

Kind of makes you think a bit don't it? Let's break it down for you. "Let the peace of Christ rule in your hearts, to which you were called in one body; and be thankful." The one body that is spoken of here is the body of Christ, the church, the peace of Christ should rule in our hearts, and we should be thankful to be a part of the body of Christ. If at any point you think to yourself that you don't want to go to church, or serve or whatever, then take a step back and look at this verse. Ask for, pray for, BEG for the peace of Christ in your heart and then move forward.

Carrying on, Colossians 3:16 says, "Let the word of Christ richly dwell within you, with all wisdom teaching and admonishing one another with psalms and hymns and spiritual songs, singing with thankfulness in your hearts to God."(NASB) The word of God is, of course the Bible. Study it, this is saying, let it become so ingrained with you that it might as well be a part of you. Use it when you are teaching or admonishing each other. This is a part where some of you might say, "Wait, I don't want to admonish anybody!" I'm not telling you that you go around yelling at everyone around you. I'm just letting you know how the Bible is telling you how to do it!

First it tells you to teach, with wisdom, which always includes the Bible, a good source of wisdom. Then it tells you to admonish, notice how it does not tell you to judge, that is reserved for God alone. How do we do that? We use psalms and songs and singing and thankfulness to God. Admonishing within the body of Christ should be a joyous event! It should be a window where we can see the peace of Christ in every face and every event!

And Colossians 3:17 says, "Whatever you do in word or deed, do all in the name of the lord Jesus, giving thanks through Him to God the Father."(NASB) There you have it, plain as day, do EVERYTHING in the name of Jesus! This means that whatever you do, you should be representing Jesus through it all.

This is particularly important to you as a Trustee. You are leaders of your church. People look up to you to show the appropriate reactions or responses to different events. They look to you for guidance, and sometimes hope when dealing with difficult times. This is the section of the Bible you go to, as a leader, to give yourself the fuel to lead in a Christ like fashion. It is not you the people look to for guidance, but the reflection of Jesus within you.

Rule Number Eight: You mean we're supposed to listen to the guy we hired to teach us?

Rule eight should be a no brainer but sadly it is this," The Pastor leads the Ministry. Ministry is the business of the Church. Trustees run the business side of the church, therefore, the Pastor LEADS the Trustees, not commands, leads. "

This is going to make a lot of church trustees and leaders FREAK OUT! You hired the pastor to teach you, and, presumably to lead the ministry of your church. Why, then do you allow some other person to lead the church leaders? The pastor can't be the chair of the trustees, he is a paid employee legally. The pastor can, however keep a very close relationship with the chair and support, or gently chastise the chair when he/she screws up. I know my pastor has no problem telling me when I'm wrong. (And I love him for it)

The main thrust of this is that we shouldn't be treating the pastor as an employee (which he/she is), but we should be treating him/her as the person that is going to feed us the Manna that we need to become better people in Christ.

I think a lot of what really gets people to thinking that they have to treat the pastor as an employee is fear. Fear that, maybe the pastor doesn't know what he's doing or that she is going to change the church to something that doesn't really resemble the impression that the particular person has for what the church should be. Fear that the pastor is going to challenge them to step out of their comfort zone and do something that they wouldn't normally do.

I've got some bad news for you. That's why you hired the pastor in the first place! He should be challenging you to do more for Christ. She should be trying to change the church into something that resembles the first century church. The day after Pentecost, the brand spanking new Christian faith gathered 3000 people in one day! Can your church say you've ever see the Holy Spirit move in such a way? Can anyone alive even say they've seen that?

That is the purpose of the church. To bring people to Christ. Would you hire an accountant to build you a deck? Of course you wouldn't . . . I hope. So why do you think that you know better how to do the pastor's job than the pastor does. This is a person that has devoted their life to building the Kingdom of God. They have studied, read and trained for the task of bringing people to a meaningful and personal relationship with God. That, presumably, is why you hired them.
Let them do their job.

This is a job that was placed on them by the Lord Himself. As always, let's look at the Bible for help. Luke 10:16 tells us this, "The one who listens to you listens to Me, and the one who rejects you rejects Me; and he who rejects Me rejects the One who sent Me." Jesus is talking to the seventy-two that He chose to go before Him and ready the way. So Jesus was talking to Preachers. Those people that would preach the Word of Jesus and God. What He's saying here is that if we listen to the Preacher we're listening to the Words of Jesus Himself. That is what a preacher is supposed to do. Tell the listeners the

Words of Christ, the message that was laid down in the Gospels two thousand years ago. The message has never changed and neither has the format.

When we listen to our pastor's preach we're hearing the words of God, we learned that in the first half of Luke 10:16. The second half is a little more dire. If we reject the preaching of our pastor, we reject Christ and by default reject God. That's a situation I'd like to avoid. But the question remains, How do we know that our preacher is preaching the Words of God?

It's pretty simple really, is he talking about the Bible? Is the Bible his number one and first source of information that he's using or is he expounding on things that have little or no relation to the Word of God. I heard someone mention once, and I'm sorry I don't remember where, "Is your preacher preaching the message of the Lord or the lord of the rings?" Meaning this, is your preacher telling the truth of the Bible, or telling the truth of the Bible watered down and spiced up with modern interpretation of that Truth?

The Bible is full of Truth. The Bible is the Word of God. God doesn't need anyone to explain Him. That's why He has the Holy Spirit. The preacher's job is to tell the Biblical truth, no filters, no apologies and ready the way for the Holy Spirit to prepare the listener's heart to receive the truth of the Bible in a way that Jesus can speak to them. That's why Luke 10:16 says, "The one who listens to you, listens to Me.".

Douglas Scaddan

Rule Number Nine: But ...but ... we wrote those!

The bylaws are not the Bible. That is the gist of rule nine; here it is for those who need clarification, "Bylaws are GUIDELINES! The Bible is the Law!"

Bylaws are a necessary evil for any church. You think I'm being hard by saying that bylaws are evil? It's true! Bylaws are our way of saying that this that or the other thing is what is important to us. However, bylaws are written by man, that is where we end up running into problems. It is the bylaws that repeatedly get churches into problems.

Okay, lets start off with what a bylaw is. A bylaw is a requirement for just about every non-profit organization that is out there. A bylaw is a set of operating instructions that prevent people from abusing the non-profit organization or creating a means of using the organization for nefarious deeds. Yes I just used those words, I've always wanted to use the word nefarious, but it generally means that we don't want people to use our churches illegally. Bylaws are supposed to provide checks and balances against that.

However, many churches also add in things that have no real connection with the operating instructions. Things like the way the order of service should be on Sunday mornings. (Seen it) Another of my favorites is that the color of the sanctuary carpet shall be Royal Blue.(The carpet again!)

The people that write these things need to keep in mind that the Bible is the only law that the church, as a religious organization, needs to follow, okay we need to follow the governmental laws too, but they don't generally get us in trouble. The church as a legal entity, a non profit organization, simply needs a bunch of operating procedures to maintain it's not for profit standing with the government.

A board of trustees, perhaps a counsel to handle the ministry side of things and the basic rules of when the various boards and committees will meet. The service lengths of each board member should be limited and spread out over time so that no one year will mean the voting in of an entirely new board. That would just be bad.

Bylaws are meant to meet the basic legal requirements to allow for a non-profit status. However, sometimes people see bylaws as a means to ensure their perfect church. To regulate and limit the powers of the pastor, whom is SUPPOSED to be the shepherd to the congregation, and the authority of the Trustees as a whole.

I will concede that in limited and rare cases power can be abused, however, a prayerful and spirit filled church shouldn't be worried about that. Also, in your bylaws should be a means to remove said abusers of power. The problem is that those checks and balances can be weighed so much to one side as to effectively tie the hands of the people that want to build the Kingdom of God.

How to fix those problems? How do we find a balance between freedom and checks and balance? That is a question that has plagued the church since it first became an organized entity back in the third or fourth century. That is a problem that needs to be approached with prayer, a lot of prayer.

Every single church is different and has a unique feel to it. Every church has it's own culture and it's own strengths and weaknesses. There is no "perfect" bylaw that I can pull out and send to you. I wish there was. The best advice that I can give to you is remembering that the Bible is the law. If your bylaw says to do something that would get in the way of something the Bible says, then do what the Bible says, and change the bylaw.

Your bylaw should also have scripture notations throughout the whole thing. It should read like a Doctoral thesis in biblical theology. The sad thing is that most bylaws are written by the people in the pews and not including the person standing at the front teaching.

Here are a couple of good scriptures that can be used in a good by-law.

Colossians 1:18, "And He is the head of the body, the church. He is the beginning, the firstborn from the dead, that in everything He might be preeminent."

1 Timothy 3:1-13, "It is a trustworthy statement: if any man aspires to the office of overseer, it is a fine work he desires to do. An overseer, then, must be above reproach, the husband of one wife, temperate, prudent, respectable, hospitable, able to teach, not addicted to wine or pugnacious, but gentle, peaceable, free from the love of money. He must be one who manages his own household well, keeping his children under control with all dignity (but if a man does not know how to manage his own household, how will he take care of the church of God?), and not a new convert, so that he will not become

conceited and fall into the condemnation incurred by the devil. And he must have a good reputation with those outside the church, so that he will not fall into reproach and the snare of the devil. Deacons likewise must be men of dignity, not double-tongued, or addicted to much wine or fond of sordid gain, but holding to the mystery of the faith with a clear conscience. These men must also first be tested; then let them serve as deacons if they are beyond reproach. Women must likewise be dignified, not malicious gossips, but temperate, faithful in all things. Deacons must be husbands of only one wife, and good managers of their children and their own households. For those who have served well as deacons obtain for themselves a high standing and great confidence in the faith that is in Christ Jesus."

Those two scriptures are by far not the only ones that you could use, but you get the idea.

Read your Bible, study it and apply it to all that you do in the church, include it in your by-laws and there can be no doubt whatsoever where the priorities of your church lie. And the first priority must be to further the Kingdom of God and the message of Christ Jesus.

Rule Number Ten: Thank you Lord that this is over!

    Rule number ten states, "Thank God for everything. If you can't find something to thank Him for, listen to your heart." Some people might read into that statement and think, "He's talking about listening to God's voice and thanking Him for that." I'm not that clever. I mean really listen to your heart. You're alive. It's that simple. Your life isn't over and you still have work to do. God's Kingdom is here and now and we work for that.

    Some people might be saying, "But my church is in shambles and we're running out of money." That's okay, because you're still alive. You're still breathing, you're heart still beats and the next day is upon you, so get up and do the work of the Lord! You should never, ever, ever quit!

    My daughter, Morgan was 4 years old and I had always told her to never quit. My wife, Tammy, and I were at a meeting at the church and a friend of ours named Frank had volunteered to watch the children while we were in this meeting, so we went to the meeting, which was just downstairs and Frank had the kids in the nursery. There's a large floor puzzle there with the alphabet on it. Morgan knew her alphabet, so she and Frank had gotten down and started doing it. One of the letters, I think it was "N" was missing. So they started to search for it. They looked and looked, after about 15 minutes Frank was ready to give up and move on to something else, but Morgan would have none of it. She enlisted the aid of the other kids and they searched for about an hour. They never found it but Morgan would not give up.

That may seem like a trivial thing to you, because you have bigger problems than a missing puzzle piece. Think of it this way, if Morgan, the 4 year old, wasn't willing to give up on a puzzle piece, should you be willing to give up on something as important as God's church?

Thank God for your beating heart because it means that you're still alive to not give up! Thank God for the trials in your life because it means that He trusts you with the really important stuff! Thank God for the person whom constantly challenges all your ideas in the Trustee meeting because it offers you a different point of view. Thank God for the people at your church that say, "But we've never done it that way.", because they remember the roots of the church. For every difficulty in your life you can find something to thank God for.

Even if you've messed up and taken the wheel away from God and things didn't work out the way that you wanted them to remember that God is in control. Give Him the praise and glory that is due to God, ask for His forgiveness and move forward, listening to that small, quiet voice that is the lord of all creation.

Do you think it's a mistake or a coincidence that the vast majority of the book of Psalms is Praise to God? Look it up yourself, as a matter of fact it would be a good thing for you to read a chapter of Psalms every day! David praises God during good times, or bad. Let's look at Psalm 22 as an example. This Psalm starts out in the first 2 verses crying out to God, his anguish is real and he is crying, "My God, my God, why have

You forsaken me?" But look then at verse 3, "Yet you are Holy." Now read the rest of the chapter, he moans and groans, but always, praises. Always.

Now on to the good stuff, when good things happen, thank God too. The biggest fear that you should have as a church leader is that at one point in your life you might stop thanking God for things. It's easy to thank God when things are going poorly. Every little thing seems to be a great gift from the Lord, but when things are going well, it would be easy to forget, or just move on.

Never forget to thank God. First on your mind should be thanking God. It should rest on your heart, waiting for an opportunity to just jump forward and praise Him for His good gifts.

Let's take a look at the coolest chapter in the Bible. Psalms 107. Here we have 4 verses in this chapter of 43 verses that say the same thing. What is this thing that is so important that it has to be repeated every 11 verses or so? "Let them give thanks to the LORD for His loving kindness, And for His wonders to the sons of men!" This is repeated in verses 8, 15, 21 and 31. What a miraculous prayer of David! He prays that other people will give thanks to the Lord! Intercessory prayer at it's best!

1 Thessalonians 2:13 says, "For this reason we also constantly thank God that when you received the word of God which you heard from us, you accepted it not as the word of men, but for what it really is, the word of God, which also performs its work in you who believe." (NASB) Thank God that people are receiving the Word of God and not the words of man. Thank God for that.

2 Timothy 1:3 says, "I thank God, whom I serve with a clear conscience the way my forefathers did, as I constantly remember you in my prayers night and day," (NASB) Here we learn that we should thank God day and night for each other. It's when we release our wants and desires and turn our faces to God in prayer and thanksgiving that we will see the true power of the Holy Spirit in our lives and in the church.

Parting Words

What to write here? I really don't have any clue whether or not any of the stuff you just read will help/benefit you. I pray that it will, but for any advice that I give you in these pages it is up to you to make the decision. Will you make decisions based upon the world and your own direction you have for the church? Or will you follow Christ and His written Word?

The word "Word" is used for two things in the Bible. The Word of God, being the words of God written down to make the Bible that we read. The Word also refers to Jesus. John 1:1 gives us what I think is the greatest description of Jesus in the world.

"In the beginning was the Word, and the Word was with God, and the Word was God"(John 1:1, NASB). We have come to view the supreme leader of our church as a friend and not too much more, we worship God, we thank God, but we really don't give Jesus too much consideration, other than the sacrifice He made on the cross. We must remember that Jesus has been around from the start, He is infinitely more complex than we can even imagine, He is with God and He is God. Think about that statement, that's enough to give you a headache!

The creator of the universe has relied on YOU to run the day to day operations of His church. It is not your church, it isn't the pastor's church, or even the people that founded it. IT. IS. JESUS'. CHURCH!

Matthew 16:18 makes this perfectly clear. "I also say to you that you are Peter and upon this rock I will build My church; and the gates of Hades will not overpower it." (Matthew 16:18, NASB) That's Jesus talking, people. To you and to me, not just to Peter. It's His church, and the gates of Hades, or Hell shall not overcome it! As long as it remains His.

God gave us free will, for good or bad, the choices we make define our relationship with Him. The very first sin was a choice that Eve made and the second was a choice that Adam made. To eat an apple (or whatever fruit it was) seems like a silly thing to punish the entire human race but it had nothing to do with the apple, it had to do with obedience; they chose to disobey God, and that was the real sin.

We regularly take the wheel from God and say, "I've got this." And God regularly says, "Okay, I'll be here when you need me." He's good like that. And when we screw up and say, "I'm sorry, please forgive me and take control in my life!" God does just that, He forgives and takes control once more. The hard part is not to take control back once we feel like we've got it under control again.

That's all just an illusion though, we never had control in the first place, God did. Jesus died so that we could have that second, third, fourth and so on chances. Never forget that. It's Jesus' church, and He is the only one that can build it. Matthew doesn't say, "I also say to you that you are Peter and upon this rock you will build the church." He says, " upon this rock I will build My church."

If you remember nothing else of these words remember this; It's Jesus' church. We're simply here to maintain it and give God the glory for the successes, or ask forgiveness for the failures of it.

Entire volumes have been written on how to lead, how to keep your team, or small group, or even your church focused on the topics or goals that have been set. But always remember this, more important than HOW you lead is WHERE you're leading to. If you and your church are all facing in the same direction, but it's at cross purposes to what God has laid out in the Bible, then you're leading is in vain.

Take a look at the Great Commandment and the Great Commission and develop a goal that is both realistic for your church, and meets the requirements that are set out in the Bible. Set your sights on that and never look back. Building the Kingdom of God is our goal, pray, study and then, only after you have done that, lead.

People, all people, have a deep hole in their souls, a longing that we try to fill with drugs, sex or any number of things that fill it for a little while. However, those things eat and rot the sides of that hole and make it larger and more empty than before. More drugs, more sex, more money. It's a deadly spiral that can only be stopped by the only thing that can fill that hole. The Love of Jesus Christ.

My daughter has a book, I can't remember what it's called now, but it says that everyone has a bucket and we can fill it with good stuff, love, kindness etc. Or we can fill it with bad stuff, rudeness, nasty words etc. Every morning we would send Morgan off to school and tell her, "Fill as many buckets as you can with good stuff today."

We can fill buckets with the Love of Christ and it will overflow! How many buckets will you fill?

THE END

On Sale Now!

From Douglas Scaddan Publishing
Faith, Hope and Love

The Janitor

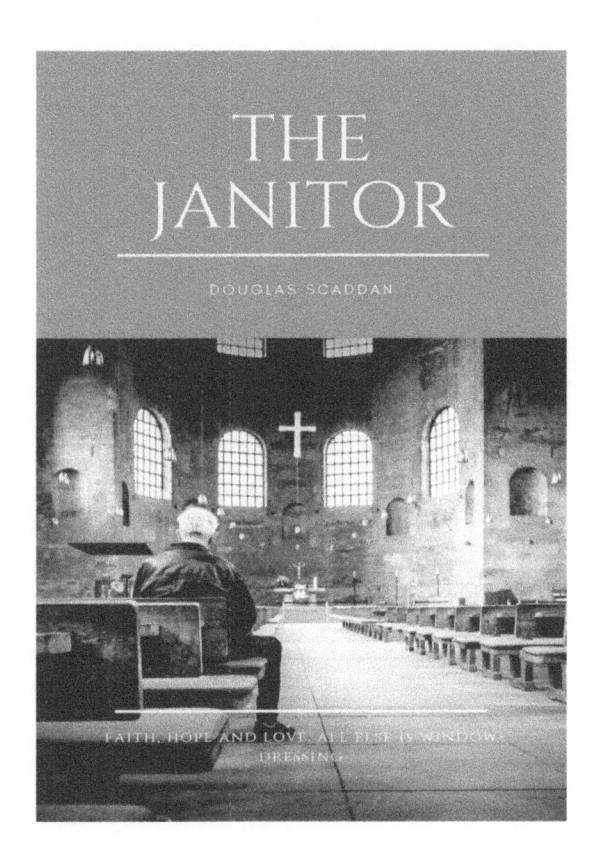

Faith, Hope and Love. . .

Everything Else is Window Dressing

About The Author

Douglas Scaddan lives in Kitchener, Ontario, Canada. He is a Developmental Service Worker for Christian Horizons, a non profit organization that is dedicated to serving people with exceptional needs.

He loves his job.

He enjoys writing about things that have meaning and maybe a little bit of controversy in them. His Soldiers of God series explores the needs of soldiers that return from service with problems they never even knew they had.

He enjoys reading, writing and working out. The latter he sometimes finds difficult to gather motivation for.